Jules the Lighthouse Dog

By P.T. Custard

Illustrations by
Ana Greer & David Pearson

To Baby "Bean":
Imagine, Believe, Be!
P.T. Custard

Black Plume Books

For those who encouraged me to be creative;
Dad, Mom, Terry, Aunt Anna Marie, and Buddy.
And for Auntie Peg, who believes in surprises.

— P.T.C.

Text © 2006 by Patricia Turner Custard
Illustrations © 2006 by Ana Greer & David Pearson
Book Design: David Pearson

Library of Congress Control Number: 2006903022

ISBN: 0-9785317-0-1

Published by:

Black Plume Books
Sunriver, OR
www.blackplumebooks.com

Printed in China by Everbest Printing Co., Ltd.
First Printing December 2006
Second Printing April 2010

See publisher's website for CPSIA information

Jules is a dog
with simply
nothing to do.

He lives at a lighthouse on a rocky cliff high above the sea. Day in and day out Jules gazes over the water. He sits. He scratches. Sometimes he naps. When he's very bored he howls his funny howl that sounds like a "Moo!"

It is a nice life but boring, and Jules wishes for more.

"I'm a clever dog," thought Jules. "There must be something that I can do. I am sure if I try hard enough I can think of a job at which I'd be the very best."

So Jules thought and puzzled as ideas raced through his head. He sat and pondered, and sat and pondered some more, until he came up with a list of possible careers. But it seemed with every job idea, there were a few, small problems.

"I could be a shiny show dog and pose proudly in the ring."

"But crowds make me nervous and I'm very camera shy."

"I love the mountains and snow and digging – I could be an avalanche rescue dog."

"But there's no snow at the lighthouse and I live by the sea."

"I could work on a farm rounding up great flocks of fluffy sheep."

"But wool makes me itch, sniff and sneeze and all that running would make me tired."

"I could be a seeing eye dog – that would be a true service to the human race."

"But I chase squirrels, birds and anything else that crosses my path."

"I could be a fearsome police dog
– now that's a job to brag about."

"I could join the circus, be a clown and travel the world."

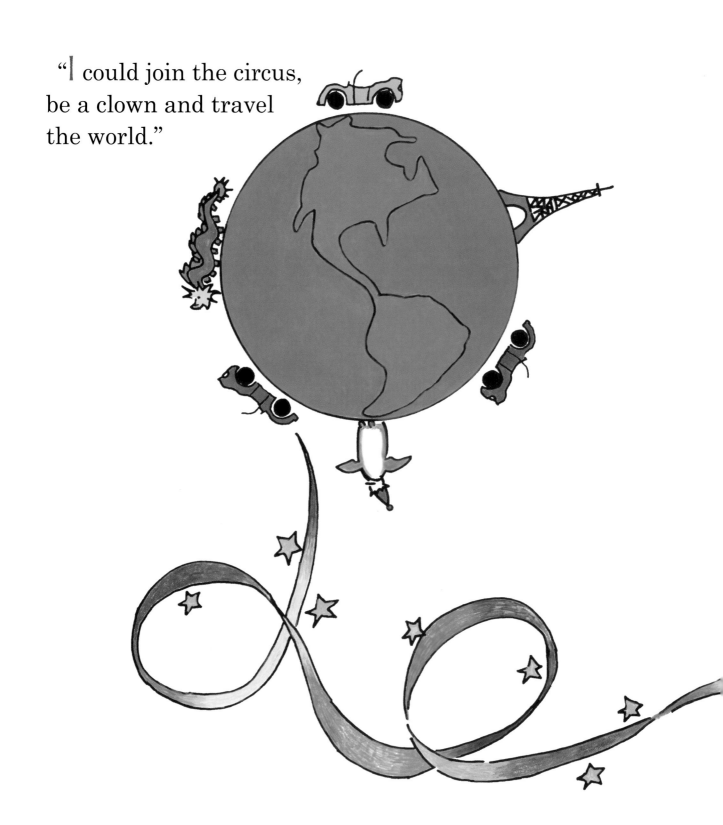

"But I'm wide and I'm large and I wouldn't fit in the clown car."

"It's no use", Jules thought. "I'm helpless and hopeless; I can't think of any job that I can do."

So Jules sat on his rock and gazed out to sea.
He moped and fretted and pouted and howled.
He despaired of ever having something more
to do. Then it happened...

The fog rolled in thick, heavy and gray. It seemed as if day had turned into night. Those traveling the waters couldn't see the lighthouse through the fog. They needed to spot the light to know if they were near land, to keep their boats from crashing into the rocky shore.

They needed something to help guide them.

THE ☗ TIMES

TODAY

JULES GETS JOB DONE!

"IT SOUNDED LIKE A COW! YOU KNOW, MOO!"

PRESIDENT PLACES CALL!

FISH HEARD IT TOO! UNCONFIRMED REPORTS

FLEET SAVED! NAVAL OFFICER CROWS "SAVED OUR SHIPS"

WEATHER SERVICE CONFIRMS YESTERDAY'S FOG WAS WORST IN 50 YEARS! JULES IS HERO!

The headlines in the papers read the next day about a heroic dog whose mighty howl kept all safe in the fog. Everyone gathered at the lighthouse to celebrate the courageous canine. Gifts, awards and a shiny medal for courage were presented to Jules - who was still not sure what the fuss was about.

"HURRAY!" the crowd shouted. "He's PERFECT for the job!" everyone agreed. "A job!?" Jules thought as the gleaming medal hung proudly round his neck. "There IS a job for me at which I would be the best!"